Lillou – the Petit Chef

and the Saucy Mission

Written by

L. Mariani

Illustrated by

L. Livi

Lillou - the Petit Chef and the Saucy Mission by Laetitia Mariani

Text and Concept © 2020 Laetitia Mariani

Illustrations Copyright © 2020 Laetitia Mariani

Published by: Color me Corsica
Illustrated by: Laura Livi – Blue Monkey Studio, Italy
Editor: Julie Jarvis
Creative consultant: Martina Weidenmo

First Edition 2020
www.MyLillou.com
www.ColorMeCorsica.com

COLOR ME CORSICA

To you,
look, listen, and learn,
and let the world surprise you.

My favorite show is about to start! Every week I watch "The Cooking Pan" starring the famous chef Paul Luton. He always says, "If you cook what you eat, you will love what you eat." I'm so excited! He's going to show us how to make his spaghetti bolognese. It sounds delicious and saucy! One pinch of salt, one pinch of black pepper, oregano, tomato sauce.... I write down every ingredient. Someone in this house is going to be happy; Thomas loves pasta! In all shapes and sizes, he loves heaps of pasta with butter and cheese or with pesto sauce and extra veggies.

This is going to be fun! But before making chef Luton's recipe, I need to come up with a twist to make it my own, as any proper chef would do.

"A twist? What's a twist?" asks Thomas with a confused look on his face.

"A twist is something unique added to the recipe to make it my very own."

"Like you do sometimes when you add rainbow colored sprinkles to your banana or chocolate chips to your roast beef." Thomas has the funniest ideas about food and his tastebuds are not always fit for a king.

"I think a twist to the pasta sounds yummy!" Thomas exclaims. "Maybe you should add marshmallows to the recipe."

"Mamma mia, blablabla!" Suddenly, we hear a loud voice traveling from the other side of the garden into our living room. As usual, it's Mr. Ventilli's voice.
Thomas and I run outside to peek through the fence like two curious little squirrels to watch Mr. Ventilli's animated face. We can't understand what his outbursts are about because he speaks in Italian. But he looks scary.

Although the summer is almost over, today is beautiful with a warm breeze. And the sky is as blue as the sea. On days like these, I like to wander outside and gather inspiration for my next recipe. Pom and I lie in the grass daydreaming of yummy dishes and occasionally look up at the little clouds passing by. Some of them look absolutely delicious, shaped like chocolate eclairs and stacks of crepes. I'm wondering if Pom sees the same shapes, or does he see juicy bones and a pile of meaty steaks?

On our way home from the field, Marco approaches us, "Hi, Lillou, what are you up to? What's on your note pad?"
"I am working on a very important project," I announce proudly.
"Is it a drawing? I'm really good at drawing, I could help you. Or is it math?

Sadly, I'm not really good at that. Now if you're talking about soccer, I'm an expert. I can teach you how to juggle the ball," says Marco getting a little carried away.
"I am working on a very important recipe," I clarify. "I'm going to make chef Luton's famous spaghetti bolognese."

Who doesn't love spaghetti bolognese? And I know it's one of Marco's favorite dishes. He always declares his love for Italian food. When Marco is very happy he makes comments like, "Mamma mia mi piace tutti i piatti della cucina italiana," making us all laugh. Then, he gets a little embarrassed and starts blushing like a cherry.

"Well, my dad makes the best spaghetti bolognese in the world," claims Marco triumphantly. "You should ask him to share his recipe."

"Your dad can't make better pasta than chef Paul Luton. It's impossible!" I respond with certainty.

"I don't know chef Luton, but my dad's pasta is definitely the best."

"Hmm, I'll make a note of that," I softly reply.

How can I ask Marco's dad for his recipe? After all, he scares me a little when he screams — it's as if someone is stepping on his toes. But if Mr. Ventilli really makes the greatest spaghetti bolognese, I need to find out his secret.

Before I can ask him, I have to secretly investigate the mystery of his screaming. I need to know if he's safe to approach.

"Detective Lillou is on a mission!" I say with much excitement.

"Yay! Special agent Thomas reporting for duty!"

"Woof woof," howls Pom joining the duo.

Today is the first day of our investigation following Mr. Ventilli's every move. We are all carefully disguised so that no one will recognize us.
A hat, a coat, and sunglasses for me. A dress, a wig, and some fancy shoes for Thomas.

A little bit of watercolor, some tape with cotton for fake little ears, and a small bow tie — there it is (et voilà)! Pom is a handsome cat look-alike. Pom's disguise is so convincing, he has already made a girlfriend, Millie, who now follows him everywhere. With everyone sufficiently dressed, the adventure can begin!

Monday (*Lundi*)
Mr. Ventilli is screaming on the phone in Italian. Something terrible must be happening!

"He is not screaming," Marco explains with a big smile on his face, "He is talking to my grandma. She doesn't hear well."

Tuesday *(Mardi)*

Hiding behind my mom's shopping cart, we hear Mr. Ventilli loudly demand, "Give me that bag!" He is trying to steal the old lady's groceries. All of a sudden, my coat gets caught in the wheel leaving me almost recognizable. "Oops, that was close!"

An instant later, my mom remarks, "Isn't he sweet? Mr. Ventilli is always insisting on helping older people carry their grocery bags."

Mr. Ventilli is yelling so loudly that the windows are shaking.
We all have to cover our ears.

"He isn't yelling, he is singing opera," Marco says laughing.

Thursday *(Jeudi)*
Something is odd. It is so quiet. Mr. Ventilli must be exhausted from all of the hollering during the week. Perhaps he is taking a nap.
"Marco, is your dad sleeping? Is he sick?" asks Thomas.

"No, today he went fishing. But funnily enough he never catches anything," Marco admits.
"My dad says that you need to be very quiet when you're fishing," I suggest to Marco with a wink.

Marco explains, "She isn't crying. She is laughing so hard that tears are streaming down her cheeks. My dad loves to tell her funny stories."

Saturday (*Samedi*)
Today, Mr. Ventilli certainly must be angry. Everyone can hear his booming voice from the street.

As I lift Thomas onto my back so he can peek through the high window, he says, "Oh, Mr. Ventilli is only watching soccer on tv, but I can't tell if his team is winning or losing."
"Oh no, Thomas, I can't see anything," Thomas's weight pulls down my hat, making me wobble and then fall onto the lawn. What a laugh! Let's just hope Mr. Ventilli didn't hear us.

Sunday (*Dimanche*)
As we follow Mr. Ventilli to the bakery, Pom and Millie beg for a treat at the entrance of the shop, putting our mission in danger.
I whisper in a panic, "Pom, Millie, come back here. Mr. Ventilli is coming."

As we all run to hide, Thomas's wig flies off his head, my glasses drop to the ground, and Pom's fake ears dangle down like earrings. What a catastrophe! In the distance Mr. Ventilli is waving his arms in the air and bellowing, but we are too far away to hear what he's shouting. He must be furious! He probably knows we were following him.

Ohlala, what are we gonna do? This investigation is a disaster. Mr. Ventilli's outbursts are not what they seem, and now I have complicated things even more!

"I really can't ask him for his recipe now! I will never know if his bolognese is truly the best," I sigh sadly.

But Thomas remains positive, "Cheer up, Lillou, maybe he didn't recognize us."

Knock, knock, knock—there is a rap at the door. Peering through the curtains, I recognize Mr. Ventilli. Now I know for certain he has seen us spying on him. Will he be angry? Will he shout? One deep breath and I open the door. Surprisingly, I find a smiley Mr. Ventilli holding a little package in one hand and the lost wig and glasses in the other.

"Hello, Lillou, I believe you dropped these items. I tried to get your attention earlier to see if you wanted some pastries, but you seemed to be in such a hurry."

Scratching my head, "Well, Thomas and I were…"

"Could it be that you were on a secret mission?" he adds winking.

"Yes, exactly," I smile with relief.

"Marco told me you were working on a spaghetti bolognese recipe, so I wanted to bring you something to make your dish taste amazing."
"Balsamic vinegar! Oh, what a wonderful addition! Thank you very much, Mr. Ventilli!"
"I only ask you for one little favor in return," Mr. Ventilli adds.

A favor in return? What kind of favor? Will he make me clean his garden? Rake the dead leaves in the winter? Wash his car? I start to get a little nervous.

"All I ask is that you let me taste your pasta once it's done," he requests.
Phew! What a relief! Feeling less intimidated I ask, "Actually, I was wondering, if you will make the bolognese sauce with me?"
"Lillou, it would be my pleasure to cook with you," replies Mr. Ventilli with a smile.

Mr. Ventilli starts explaining the recipe: "While cutting the onion, king of the vegetables, do not be sad even though it may make you cry. It is crunchy, hot, and spicy when eaten raw, but it is also sweet and caramelized when cooked low and slow. Its strong scent will tickle your nose, putting a spell on you. It is every chef's magical jewel."

Then, Mr. Ventilli continues by singing the recipe just like his mom taught him. I must admit, Mr. Ventilli is patient, kind, and very funny. His loud singing makes Thomas curious and he rushes into the kitchen.

"One, two, three,
Onions have a dance party.
Four, five, six,
In the oil they twirl and mix.

Seven, eight, nine,
Beef, tomato, it is time.
Here comes ten,
and you did well,
Add the spices,
Mmm that's smell!

My oh my this was fun,
Let it simmer,
then you're done!"

"Alright, Lillou," says Mr. Ventilli, "I think I can leave you to finish the recipe by yourself. I have to run some errands, but I will see you again very shortly."

"What about your twist, Lillou? I still think you should add marshmallows to your sauce! It would taste so delicious!" Thomas reminds me with a big dreamy face. Marshmallows? Of course! Thomas is a genius! I squeeze him and kiss his cheek as I exclaim, "I know what my twist is going to be!"

"Ahoooooooo!" howls Pom.
"No, Pom, not marshmallows! But a little bit of heavy cream."

Before cooking, here is the
list of the cooking materials required:

An apron

A chopping board

A knife

A measuring cup

A garlic press

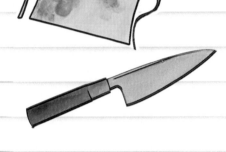

A spatula

A saucepan

A large cooking pot

A strainer

And, like any head chef, an assistant is necessary.
Ask your parents or an adult to assist you. Remember,
before starting to cook, make sure you wash your hands.

LA RECETTE
SPAGHETTI BOLOGNESE

1 onion

1 can (15oz)
of tomato sauce

1lb (500g) of ground beef

1 clove of garlic

1 tsp of salt

1 pinch of black pepper

1 tbsp of balsamic vinegar

1 tbsp of olive oil

(*) FOR
LILLOU'S SPICE
SEE
TIPS AND TRICKS

1 tbsp Lillou's spice

1/4cup (25ml) of heavy cream

1lb (500g) spaghetti uncooked

1/2 cup shredded mozzarella cheese

1. On the chopping board, cut off the top of the onion keeping the root intact; it'll keep the onion together as you chop (A). Turn the onion to rest on the flat end and slice it in half vertically (B). Now peel the skin off the onion (C).

(A)   (B)   (C)

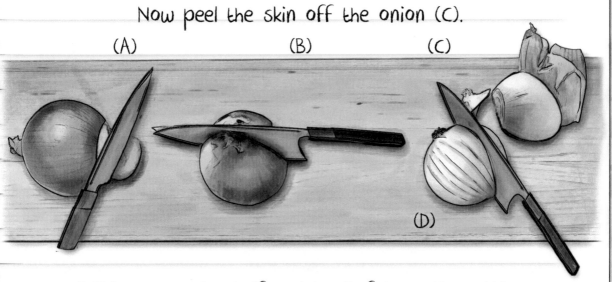

(D)

2. Take one onion half and lay it flat on the cutting board. Holding the root end, carefully cut horizontally. Still holding the onion root, slice vertically (D) until you reach the root. Now do the same with the other half.

3. Peel the skin off the garlic (A).
Put the garlic inside the
garlic press and
squeeze hard (B). (C)
Then put the crushed garlic aside. (C).

(A)

(B)

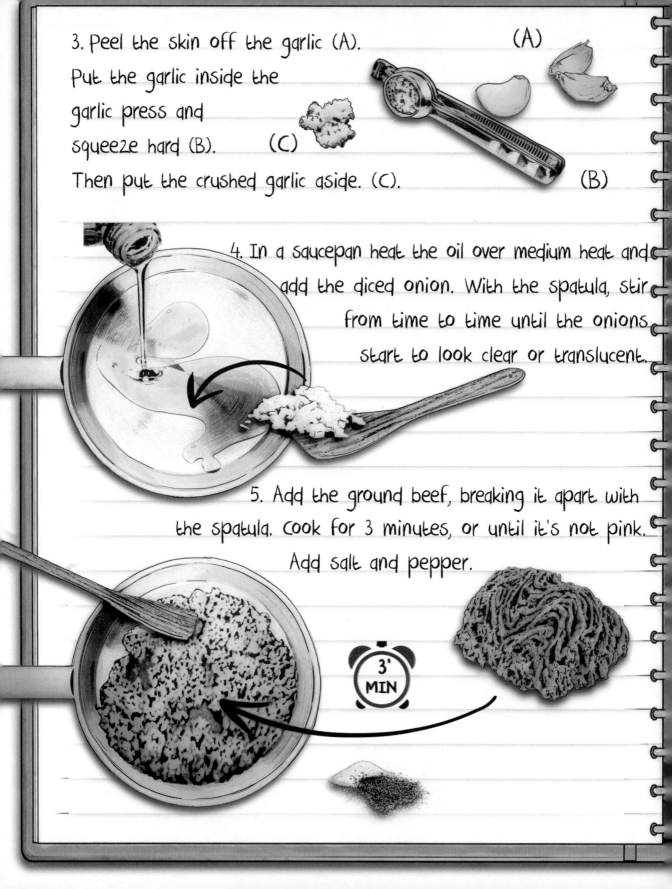

4. In a saucepan heat the oil over medium heat and
add the diced onion. With the spatula, stir
from time to time until the onions
start to look clear or translucent.

5. Add the ground beef, breaking it apart with
the spatula. Cook for 3 minutes, or until it's not pink.
Add salt and pepper.

3'
MIN

6. Add the tomato sauce (A), the crushed garlic (B), Lillou's spice (C), and the balsamic vinegar (D). Stir well. Reduce the heat to medium/low. Cover and cook for 20 minutes.

(A)   (B)   (C)   (D)

7. Once the sauce is ready, add the heavy cream and stir.

8. In the Large cooking pot, bring water to a boil and cook the pasta as directed on the package.

9. When the pasta is cooked, mix it into the sauce and carefully stir.

10. Serve and garnish the top with shredded mozzarella or your favorite cheese.

TIPS and TRICKS

You don't have time to make your own tomato sauce? Start the recipe from step 5 and modify step 6 by using your favorite pre-made marinara sauce.

You want to make a bolognese without beef? Replace it with ground turkey or any ground meat alternative.

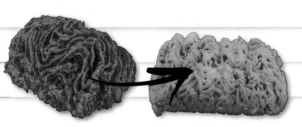

You don't want to use dairy? Replace the heavy cream with any milk alternative.

LILLOU'S SPICE

Blend 1 teaspoon of each of the following: oregano, basil, and thyme. Add 2 bay leaves - voilà! Lillou's spice!

The pasta is done and I am eager to find out if Mr. Ventilli will like it. As we all gather around the dinner table, the first one to grab a fork is Mr. Ventilli with an intense look on his face. It is the same look chef Luton has when he is about to taste a new dish. It is business.

"Let's all find out how good your spaghetti bolognese is. Lillou, your sauce is a little different than mine…hmm…creamy…."

Then, Mr. Ventilli stops talking and starts chewing his food with his eyes closed.
I am horrified. Silence. Not a word. It's so silent you can hear a pin drop.
He doesn't like it. Maybe I ruined his recipe. Mr. Ventilli is never quiet, ever!

"MAGNIFICO! Your bolognese is MAGICAL! What wonderful flavors! And your twist makes it so soft and creamy!" he cries joyfully.

"Lillou, your pasta dish is so good. You made Mr. Ventilli speechless for a moment," says Thomas astonished.

"I guess there can be more than one great spaghetti bolognese. But more importantly, Thomas, I think we solved the mystery: Mr. Ventilli is not an angry person after all. I think he's loud because he is very passionate."

"Come on everyone, let's grab our plates and enjoy this delicious pasta!" Mr. Ventilli thunders.
"Yay!!! Bon appetit!" We all shout back in unison.

Fin

(The End)

If you are wondering what happened to Pom and Millie, with Pom's true identity revealed, poor Millie was a little heartbroken.
But after spending a week together, they seem to have become the best of friends anyway.
Who says cats and dogs can't get along?

Lillou's Dictionary

Monday = *Lundi* [lahn-dee]

Tuesday = *Mardi* [mahr-dee]

Wednesday = *Mercredi* [mair-cruh-dee]

Thursday = *Jeudi* [zhuh-dee] the **zh** is pronounced like the "**s**" in treasure

Friday = *Vendredi* [vawn-druh-dee]

Saturday = *Samedi* [sah-muh-dee]

Sunday = *Dimanche* [dee-mawn-sh]

There it is = *Et voilà* [eh voua-lah]

One = *Un* [ahn]

Two = *Deux* [duh]

Three = *Trois* [trou-ah]

Four = *Quatre* [ka-trh]

Five = *Cinq* [sahn-k]

Six = *Six* [sees]

Seven = *Sept* [set]

Eight = *Huit* [wu-eat]

Nine = *Neuf* [nuff]

Ten = *Dix* [dees]

Thank you for coming along, see you in the next adventure!
Always remember to dream big - you can be whatever you want to be!

Find me on social media

facebook.com/LillouThePetitChef
Instagram.com/myLillou
www.mylillou.com

Made in United States
Troutdale, OR
11/29/2024

25490945R00033